The Bee's Sneeze

Written by

Lucy Davey

Illustrated by

Katz Cowley

With love for Hope, our darling little bumblebee xx
– L.D.

For my beautiful Aunt (& 'other Mum') Jen
All the colours in this book are for every rainbow
you blaze across the sky and have woven into our hearts x
– K.C.

This edition published in the UK in 2021 by Scholastic Children's Books
Euston House, 24 Eversholt Street, London NW1 1DB
A division of Scholastic Ltd
www.scholastic.co.uk
London – New York – Toronto – Sydney – Auckland – Mexico City – New Delhi – Hong Kong

First published in 2016 by Scholastic New Zealand Limited

ISBN 978 0702 30632 7

Printed in China

1 3 5 7 9 10 8 6 4 2

Papers used by Scholastic Children's Books are made from wood grown
in sustainable forests and other controlled sources.

On Tootletuff Hill,
figliciously big,
grew fruit-i-ful groves
of the Tootletuff fig.

One day, a lorikeet
swooped for a feed,
flew far away ...

and pooped out a seed.

The seed hit the ground
in Willowomp Wood,
near Crocodile Swamp,
where the soil was good.

Soon, from the seed
grew the teensiest plume
of a shoot,
then a plant,
then a Tootletuff bloom.

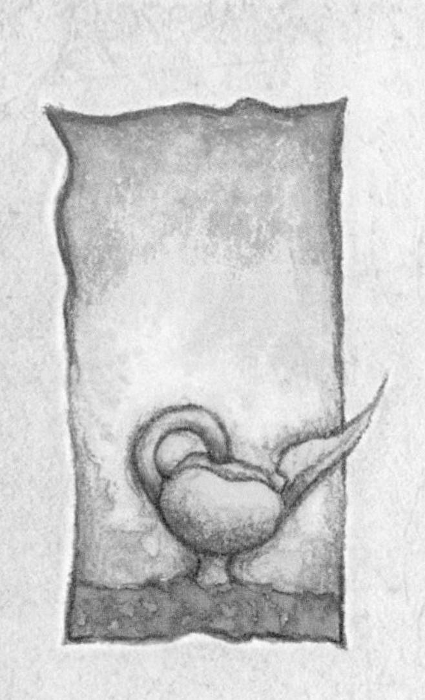

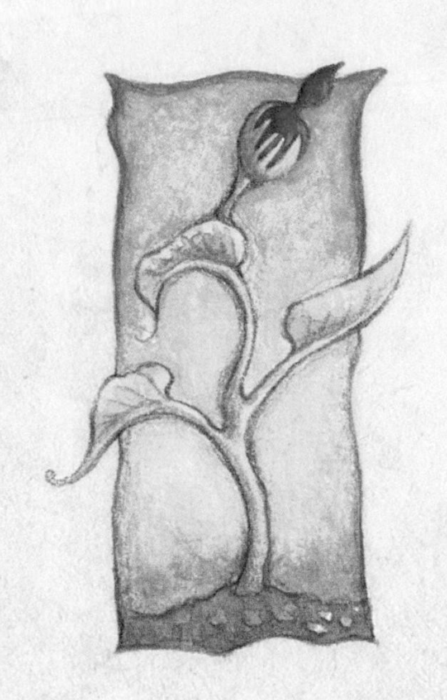

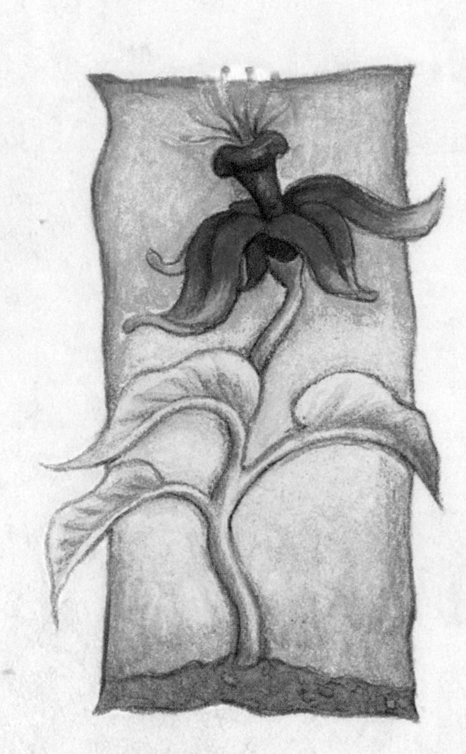

Buzzy McBee was busy on high.
The lovely new flower attracted her eye.

“My!” said Buzz, with a loop-da-loo flip.
“I’ll zip right down for a nectary nip.”

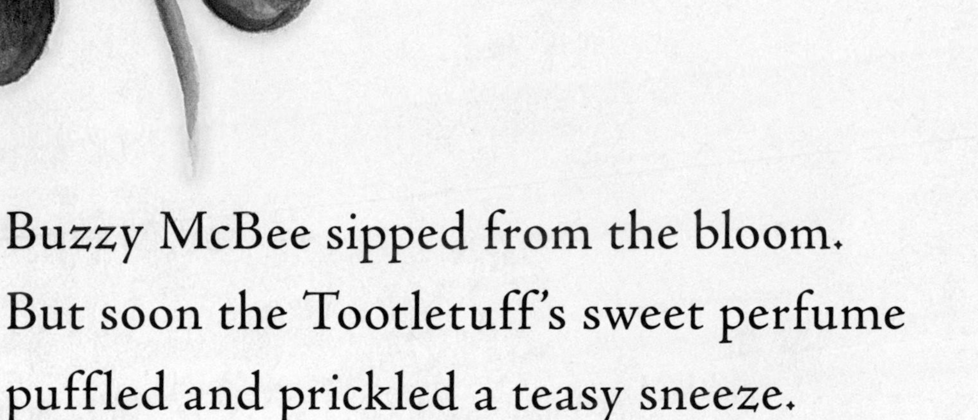

Buzzy McBee sipped from the bloom.
But soon the Tootletuff's sweet perfume
puffled and prickled a teasy sneeze.

"Uh-oh!" cried Buzzy McBee.

"I smell a whiff, a tickle-ish sniff,
I'll *squeeze* the sneeze inside!"

So Buzzy McBee wobbled her knees,
but still that teasy sneeze came breezing.

Jiggling and joggling like kids at the zoo,
it grew till it blew with a loud ...

AH-CHOO!

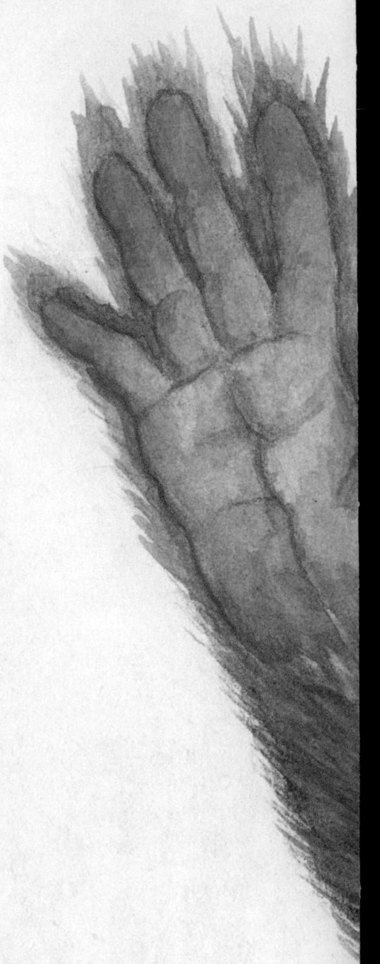

Rumbly-tumbly, head-over-end,
Buzzy McBee bumped into a friend.

"Bless you!" said Monkey Minx.

"Thank you," said Buzzy, "but help me, please,
to shift this flower that's making me sneeze."

"Sure!" said Monkey, and dug out the bloom.
But soon the Tootletuff's sweet perfume
swirled and curled a teasy sneeze.

"Uh-oh!" cried Monkey Minx.

"I smell a whiff, a tickle-ish sniff,
I'll *squeeze* the sneeze inside!"

Monkey Minx winked and blinked,
Buzzy McBee wobbled her knees –
but still that teasy sneeze came breezing.

Bubbling and boiling like bushman's brew,
it grew till it blew with a loud ...

AH-CHOO!

Bumbling backwards, Monkey and Buzz,
landed *kersploof* on a friendful of fuzz.

"Bless you!" said Barefoot Bear.

"Thank you," said Monkey, "but help us, please,
to carry this flower that's making us sneeze."

"Sure!" said Barefoot, toting the bloom.
But soon the Tootletuff's sweet perfume
wafted and whirled a teasy sneeze.

"Uh-oh!" cried Barefoot Bear.

"I smell a whiff, a tickle-ish sniff,
I'll *squeeze* the sneeze inside!"

Barefoot Bear pulled on his hair,
Monkey Minx winked and blinked,
Buzzy McBee wobbled her knees –
but still that teasy sneeze came breezing.

Like ants in the pants of a kangaroo,
it grew till it blew with a loud ...

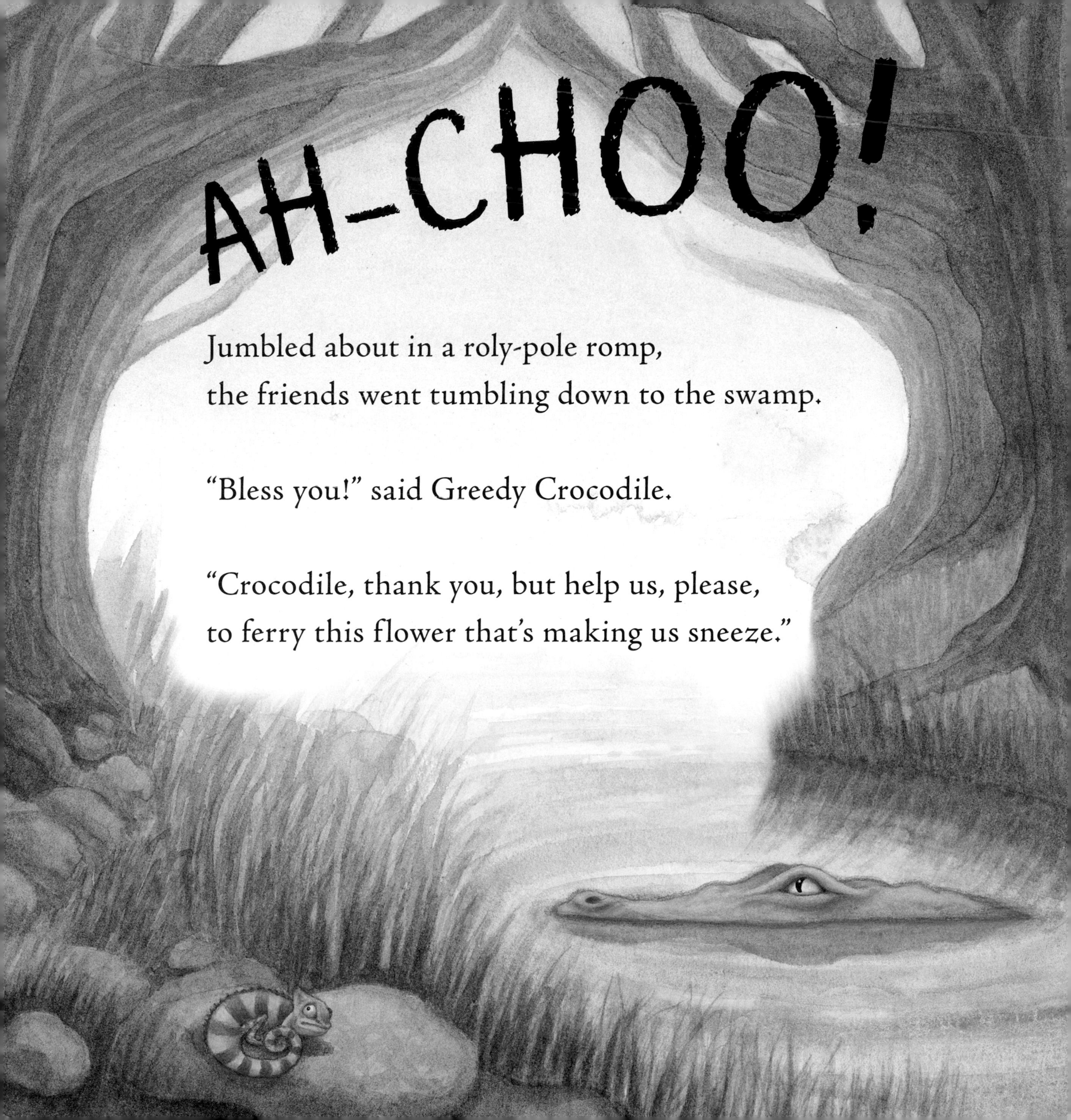

AH-CHOO!

Jumbled about in a roly-pole romp,
the friends went tumbling down to the swamp.

"Bless you!" said Greedy Crocodile.

"Crocodile, thank you, but help us, please,
to ferry this flower that's making us sneeze."

"Sure!" said Crocodile. "Hop on my back.
I'll have you across the swamp, quick-quack."

But Lizzie-ma-Lou was curled on a rock.
She stirred when she heard the words of the Croc.

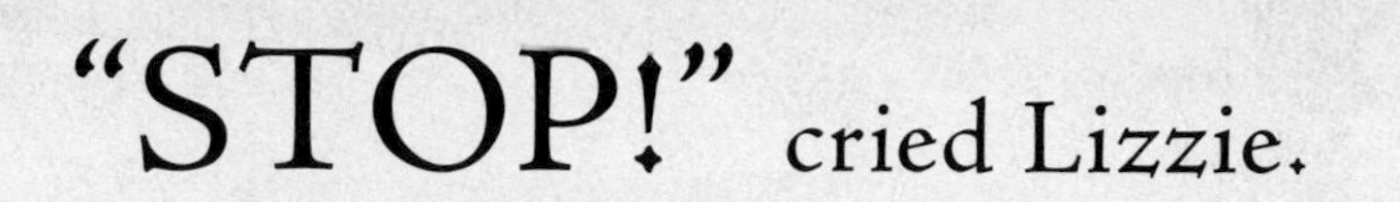

"STOP!" cried Lizzie.

"Watch out! Have fear!

He'll gobble you all!

But here's an idea …

"Let's make a chain, and swing in a line

over the swamp, like riding a vine."

So, linking with Lizzie, they **swung** with the bloom …

but soon the Tootletuff's sweet perfume
wheezed and tweezed a teasy sneeze.

"**Uh-oh!**" cried Lizzie-ma-Lou.

"Now *I* smell a whiff, a tickle-ish sniff!
I'll *squeeze* the sneeze inside."

Lizzie-ma-Lou turned herself blue,
Barefoot Bear pulled on his hair,
Monkey Minx winked and blinked,
Buzzy McBee wobbled her knees –
but still that teasy sneeze came breezing.

Crocodile grinned,
"There's nought you can do.
That sneeze will explode!
Just wait ..."

AH-CHOO!

Hungrily watching them fall and flap,
Crocodile opened his mouth and ...

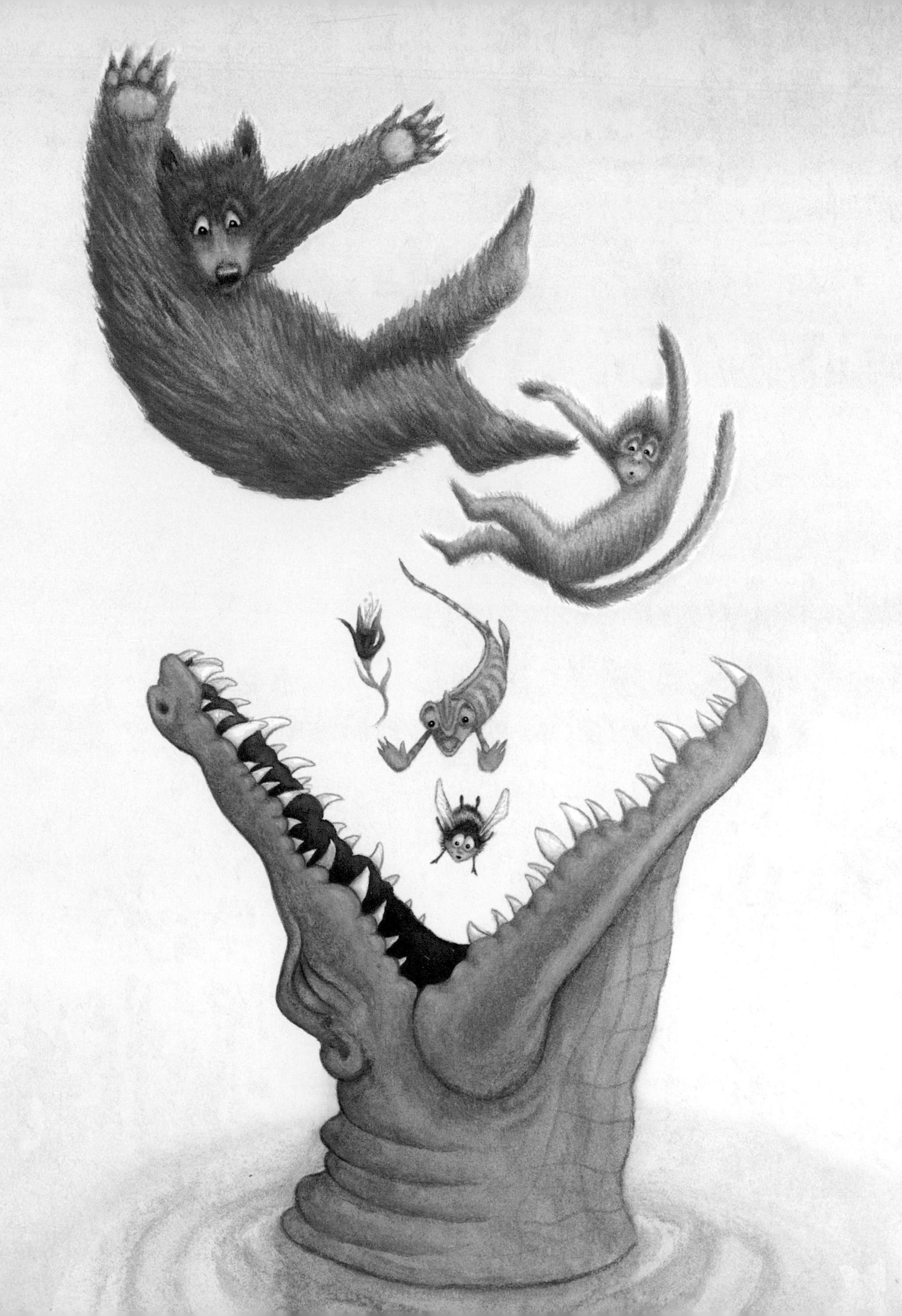

Buzzy McBee, Monkey Minx,
Barefoot Bear and Lizzie-ma-Lou
were swallowed up whole!
(In one gulp, too.)

"Yum-hum!" Crocodile smiled, but soon,
from deep inside, that Tootletuff bloom
prickled and tickled a teasy sneeze –
like a fearsome volcano that fizzled and grew,
until it exploded and blew ...

AH-CHOOO!

Out came the friends – and the Tootletuff too!

Buzzy, Lizzie, Monkey and Bear
were mightily glad to be out in fresh air!
They romped from the swamp with a zip and a stomp,
while Crocodile gave them a glowering glare.

And what of the bloom that was thrown to the sky?
'Twas caught by a lorikeet flying by!

It slipped from her clutch over Tootletuff Hill,
landing roots down, and is growing there still.